"Freedom and liberty for all!"

Little Patriot Press® is a registered trademark of Salem Communications Holding Corporation

Cataloging-in-Publication data on file with the Library of Congress
ISBN 978-1-62157-517-7

Published in the United States by
Little Patriot Press
An imprint of Regnery Publishing
A Division of Salem Media Group
300 New Jersey Ave NW
Washington, DC 20001
www.RegneryKids.com
www.Peanuts.com

Manufactured in the United States of America
10 9 8 7 6 5 4 3 2 1

Books are available in quantity for promotional or premium use. For information on discounts and terms, please visit our website: www.Regnery.com.

Distributed to the trade by
Perseus Distribution
250 West 57th Street
New York, NY 10107

Hooray for Liberty, Charlie Brown!

QUEEN LUCY'S
CLUB HOUSE

ADMISSION 5¢

Peanuts created by Charles M. Schulz

Written by Tracy Stratford Illustrated by Tom Brannon

Little Patriot Press

"We've got to come up with something fun to do," Charlie Brown announced.

"Hey, everybody, I've got an idea—let's build a club house!" Lucy announced. "I'll be the supervisor!"

"Supervisor?" Sally asked.

"Okay, I'll go get a hammer," Franklin said.

"And I'll get some nails!" Charlie Brown said.

In no time, everyone was busy—drawing plans, gathering tools, collecting boards. Everyone except Lucy, that is. She was supervising!

"Careful with that board, Patty!" she barked from her chair. "Franklin, Charlie Brown needs more nails! Snoopy, bring me more lemonade!"

"Hit the nail, not your thumb, blockhead!"
Lucy scolded Charlie Brown. "Hey, Sally,
you missed a spot."

"Who does Lucy think she is—queen of the club house?" Marcie said.

Lucy perked up. "Did someone say 'queen'? I like that idea!"

After they finished, Franklin declared, "This is the world's best club house. Good job, team!"

"Our next job is—lunch!" Linus said. "We'll come back afterward to play in it."

When they returned, Linus yelled up to Lucy, "Will you please toss us the ladder?"

"No, I will not!" said Lucy, who was now wearing a crown on the top of her head.

"I've decided to be queen of this club house and you must pay me if you want to play up here! Five cents please!" Lucy declared. "Schroeder, do you want to come up and be my king? No charge for kings!"

"Wait a minute—we built this club house together!" Franklin said. "It belongs to all of us. You can't do this!"

"Too bad! Kings and queens get to do whatever they want, whenever they want," Lucy said. "Oh Schroeder, are you coming up?"

"This is an outrage, Lucy van Pelt!" Marcie huffed.

"Good grief," Charlie Brown said.

Linus sighed. "You know what this reminds me of?" he said. "The people who lived in America during colonial times. We studied them."

He continued, "The English king ruled the American colonies back then, and wanted them to pay lots of taxes because he said he protected them. But he kept on adding more rules and more taxes."

"What did the colonists do?" Sally asked.

Linus answered, "The colonists became very unhappy so they protested! They told him they refused to pay money when they didn't have a voice—'no taxation without representation' was their motto."

"No taxation without representation! Hey, that's what Lucy is doing to us!" Sally said.

"We should all have a say in how we run our own club house! She can't tell US what to do!" Franklin protested.

"She is not the queen of US!" Marcie added.

"How did they get the king to stop?" Peppermint Patty asked.

"The colonists just said 'no'!" Linus explained. "They wrote a declaration—the Declaration of Independence!

"They declared they would not pay him unless they had a say in the decisions being made in America. They decided they did not want a king at all!"

"That's what we are going to do!" Charlie Brown said.

"We are going to write down the rules for OUR club house," said Linus.

"And tell Lucy she can't tell us what to do!" yelled Patty.

"And the biggest rule is—nobody has to pay to play in the club house we built together!" they all cheered.

Back at the club house, Lucy sipped her tea all alone.

"It's kind of lonely being queen," Lucy sighed.

All of a sudden, Lucy heard noises coming from down below.

"Lucy, we demand you hear us!" the gang shouted.

Charlie Brown threw their declaration into the club house window. "Our club house is FREE and so are WE! Liberty for all! Liberty from Lucy!" they chanted.

Lucy dropped the ladder down.

"Come on up, everyone!" she said. "I guess you're right. This club house belongs to all of us, and no one has to pay to play in it!"

Lucy continued, "Everyone will have a say and a voice from now on!"

"Even you, Charlie Brown!" she added. "Freedom and liberty for all!"

Hooray for liberty!

Hooray for Liberty

Why did America need a Declaration of Independence?

The United States of America was known as British America before its independence. The group of 13 colonies was ruled by Great Britain for more than 150 years begining in the early 17th century.

In the 1750s and 1760s, Britain and France were at war in North America over which country would dominate it and its rich resources. France was helped in the fighting by some American Indian tribes. Many colonists, including a young George Washington, fought alongside the British as subjects of the king. Britain won, but the war left the country with heavy debts.

The king decided to assert more control over the colonies and, without their input, to tax them more. One new law prevented colonists from moving further west; another raised taxes on sugar to help pay for the colonies' defense. These steps upset many colonists. But in 1765, Parliament angered them even more by passing the Stamp Act, which taxed shipping, tavern licenses, newspapers, and other products and services through the sale of special stamps. The colonists began to protest in the streets and to boycott English goods.

The colonists were not happy with King George and Great Britain. The leaders of the 13 colonies got together in Philadelphia to figure out what to do. The Second Continental Congress wanted to inform the king of how people were feeling, and what they wanted done.

The Declaration of Independence was written because the colonists had suffered years of oppression by the king of England—he sent his British Redcoats to attack American subjects. Britain also denied them representation in government and unfairly taxed their sugar, molasses, and tea.

Who wrote the Declaration of Independence?

The Second Continental Congress met in Philadelphia in May 1776. In June, delegates from Virginia proposed a resolution of independence. Congress did not act on it right away; instead it appointed a committee to draft a formal declaration of independence that would explain the colonists' reasons and justification for breaking away from Great Britain. The committee included Benjamin Franklin of Pennsylvania, John Adams of

Massachusetts, and 33-year-old Thomas Jefferson of Virginia. Thomas Jefferson was asked to write the actual "letter" because he was such a good writer.

Jefferson wrote the draft in seventeen days with the assistance of Franklin and Adams. After some changes were made by the rest of the committee, they presented it to Congress on June 28, 1776.

What did the Declaration of Independence say?

The Second Continental Congress decided it was time for the colonies to officially declare their independence. This meant that they were breaking away from British rule. They would no longer be a part of the British Empire and would fight for their freedom.

The Declaration of Independence contained important points the congressional representatives of the 13 colonies wanted King George to know.

It first said why they were writing this declaration.

It told the king what they believed made good government.

It listed all the bad things that the king had done to the colonies. It stated the colonies had rights that they were willing to fight for.

It declared the colonies free and independent from Britain. Basically, the Declaration of Independence declared war against King George and Great Britain.

This is the most famous line from the Declaration of Independence:

"We hold these truths to be self-evident, that all men are created equal, that they are endowed by their Creator with certain unalienable Rights, that among these are Life, Liberty and the Pursuit of Happiness."

The Declaration of Independence was signed by 56 congressional representatives on July 4, 1776.

After the signing, the document was sent to a printer to make copies. Copies were sent to all the colonies, where the declaration was read aloud in public and published in newspapers. A copy was also sent to the British government.

On July 4, 1776, the Congress officially adopted the final version of the Declaration of Independence. This day is still celebrated in the United States as Independence Day.

The most famous version of the Declaration of Independence is on display at the National Archives in Washington, D.C.